PRELUDES OF LOVE

BY

NINDITA JANHABEE SWARO

ISBN 978-93-5438-294-9

Published in India 2020 by Pencil

A brand of
One Point Six Technologies Pvt. Ltd.
123, Building J2, Shram Seva Premises,
Wadala Truck Terminal, Wadala (E)
Mumbai 400037, Maharashtra, INDIA
E connect@thepencilapp.com
W www.thepencilapp.com

AUTHOR BIOGRAPHY

Anindita Janhabee Swaro, 18, is an internationally published poet and story writer. Putting her heart and soul into literature, Anindita has been writing poetry since she was just 11. She is the winner of the Newark and Sherwood international poetry contest 2017. She has two of her poetry collections published under Amazon's Createspace and a short-story in the U.S. based anthology - Circus of Indie artists: true love edition. She hails from the state of Odisha, India, and is a student English Honours at the very reputed Ravenshaw University, Odisha. Anindita aspires to be a successful poet and novelist in future.

Anindita's other collections –

Flames of a Burning Heart

Snowflakes

Reach Anindita at Instagram (@Anindita_Janhabee) and Facebook (https://www.facebook.com/AninditaWritings)

CONTENTS

PREFACE 6

ADIEU 7

SUNDERING PETALS 8

OUR FIRMAMENT 10

CHASING YOU 11

SYNONYM OF SILENCE 12

KEPT WAITING 13

HIS POETRY 14

AN IMMATURE GIRL 15

A ROSE LIKE SMILE 16

REDEFINE YOUR PAIN 17

RISE OF A FALLEN STAR 19

ABSURDITIES OF LONELINESS 21

THE LABYRINTH 22

THE BREEZE 23

COBWEBS OF SILENCE 24

THE BRIDGES 25

THE EPISTLE 26

RECALL 27

ANOTHER CUP 28

THERE WAS A GUY	29
PRELUDES OF LOVE	30
ETHEREAL	34
UNHEARD EUPHONY	35
ARRIVAL OF THE DEPARTURE	36
THE JOY FOREVER	37
WALK A MILE IN MY SHOES	38
THE ORCHID OF LOVE	39
HALF PENNED VERSE	40
PARALLEL UNIVERSE	41
THE BOOK	42
NIGHT VISIONS	43
THE HEART IN TRANCE	44
POTENTIAL MIST	45
IN REMEMBRANCE	47

PREFACE

Poetry springs up when emotions override one's heart. They're pure pieces of emotions, closely adjoined to feelings, perspectives and vivid descriptions of colours and lights that everyone isn't able to see.

This collection of poetry is enthusiastic about the different aspects of love. Every poem depicts a unique story, follows an interesting road to reach the unknown destination. On the way, however, feelings rise, fall, swipe and stand tall. We win and lose but even when lost, we haven't really lost.

The poems best describe the fact that feelings are pure and even when they're true, sometimes they can't be requited. Some emotions are meant to let them be the way they are, not bothering if they're reflected in the same way by the other person. They take their aim to unite with the other person but on failing they aren't in distress. Rather, they keep longing and stay – stay till a human life lasts and maybe a little more than that.

ADIEU

Decorum included the wax candles
Fairy lights brightened up the walls
As majestic as the stars to the sky
His eyes glittered till falls

His touch on my arms and my face
Our relation could never be a disgrace

Respect, love and hope were a grandeur
Achievements and ambitions marked our splendour

However inconsistent be our virtue
Inconsistency in presence called for an adieu.

SUNDERING PETALS

The randomly lying petals
Of the bouquet of flowers
Belonged to a soul
And the heart of love showers

Tenderness on touch
Softly they drifted with the sea waves
Damped on the soil ruthlessly
They didn't know what path destiny paves

The setting sun must've been the witness
I picked them up in misery
For they looked like flowers to the rest
To me, they were an ecstatic heart's injury

The innocent petals sobbed
Some existed, some washed away
In the ocean of love
Like left-over in the astray

Preludes of Love

Wanderings of the yellow petals
Heart's secrets decouple
Just like love they float down
Ramblings of the broken soul.

OUR FIRMAMENT

The firmament we share is boundless
And so is the vibrant truth and transparency
There have been a million good memories, you remember?
And a million more of discrepancy

It's been years that I'm writing for you
But never did my words fluctuate much
I've penned almost all your versions I've met
Still, I'm so curious if I've missed one of such?

Now let go of the agony, my love
That gyre like feeling fulminates to pollute
Meet me in reality, under this ambient firmament
For I can't hold the poesy silence for another minute.

CHASING YOU

Ever since then, I'm chasing
Chasing dreams, chasing relations
Chasing my deepest desires
That led me to you
To follow your footsteps
And to achieve pursuits
To chase again what makes me happy
I keep chasing until I am tired
And I again end up visiting you
Once again, another time
To chase the wonders, beliefs
And to travel into another world
Only with you.

SYNONYM OF SILENCE

Sometimes words don't get
Their way out
They're just caged in
And the pen shivers
Along with unvarnished nails
But fails to find
The right untrodden path
Out to the white field
From within the heart
And they're afraid
For they desire secrecy
The ink then flows
But only as blots
Words after all
Are powerful creatures
Holding their heads high
In the end defend the ink…

KEPT WAITING

Behind the tears of those brown eyes
Lied a little ray of hope
For things didn't favour
She kept waiting with the lamp

The letter box is empty
And so is her soul
Light fades and darkness is up
As she's waiting

Next rise of the world
Was a flower's bloom
Opening the letterbox in hurry
All she found was emptiness

Darkness arrives again
Yet another hope rises
With the little oil and hope
She kept waiting…

HIS POETRY

His poetry reflects her eyes
His chamomile tea starts her day
His arms soothe her soul
And his smiles mark her way

His words make her swing
His hands, caress her hair
His purity throws away her pain
And his heart mirrors that she's fair.

AN IMMATURE GIRL

I wish to be that immature girl
Who'd hold you back
Close her eyes and cry
Yell and throw tantrums
And force you to stay back
Unmoved by the responsibilities
Untouched by the obligations
Neither bound to understand situations
Nor delighted to experience silence
I wish to be that immature girl
Who'd clutch onto your hands tight
Without a second thought of others
Selfishly cling onto your heart.

A ROSE LIKE SMILE

The sound of her voice
Has an euphonious beauty
The delicacy in her soul
Has an innocent purity

Her beautiful personality
Has an amazing charm
Her kind mindset
Can never cause harm

She has got resemblance
To a tree
Who sucks pain and sadness
And makes me free

A friend so close yet untouched
I've gotten so far
Beyond my reach
She's like a star.

REDEFINE YOUR PAIN

Look into your life with heads high
It's your heart which is broken
You still hold your values and morals
Powerless, you don't stand awoken

Look into the art of pain
It's not just tears that you hold
That's more about regaining strength
Waking up once again, your heart of gold.

Look into the beauty of torments
How tough does it seem to move on?
Shattering painfully into pieces is indeed
A little ache and melancholy that's hardly ever gone

Look deep inside, at the bright dullness of life
Calmly it disintegrates your mind
Torn letters, diaries and notes put into fireplace
The brightest star made you blind

Look on the serenity of silence around
The flowers are no more colourful to you
Abusing the pretty fine palm creases
After they intertwined in the night of blue

Preludes of Love

Look on the greater side of pain
It reinforces your feelings if true
Hold on to them for they're little miracles
Even if unaccepted, they don't degrade in value.

RISE OF A FALLEN STAR

The sky, quite cloudy
And she almost unknown
To my innocent keen eyes
Her glorious spark she'd shown

Empty without makeover
Her eyes beautified with spects
She glowed with simplicity
Her emotions with lonely tests

Music turns on
As I step towards her
Those steps together
Made us a beginner

Now we held hands
Smiles were the decorum
A perfume of closeness
And we tried whispering some

Names exchanged and then
Was the time erasing hunger
Big foodie she was
But her heart was in sombre

Preludes of Love

Flavours spoke innocence
Liquid like our hobbies matched
She wrote beautifully each time
While I made a glance she fetched

Shaking hands the next day we met
As I marched to erase her scar
Gentle she was, her words so beautiful
That day of meeting
Marked the rise of a fallen star.

ABSURDITIES OF LONELINESS

I fall short of words
I see myself as sharply changing swords

As drastic as sea waves, in every day's action
I now find a different reflection

Of myself, every morning in the mirror
I'm changing, unafraid of the horror

And the cause isn't you but me
That I think twice before sharing, you see!

And I stop thrice before walking ahead
I fail numerable times, crying on my bed

I'm afraid of strangers more than ever
Never had I been this clever

And I've grown tall as a mountain now
Lost all the innocence, somehow.

THE LABYRINTH

I am here
Driven off by words
Uncertainly something bonding
Right there, inside your heart
As the star rests there
Twinkling and then vanishing
In the labyrinth of your eyes
Once where I lost myself
Caught the star with shaking palms
Cried a tear for
There wasn ’ t my name
It shone with emptiness
And I set it out free
Along with myself
From the wonderland
Where I had been lost for ages
Out to reality
Am here, once again
Shaping the bond
Though my name unwritten
For now, and ages,
When I close my eyes …

THE BREEZE

It might be just a blow of wind
Or an entire world of memories
Rushing past my face
Bringing thrills down my spine
And wait…
It has a different miracle
Of bringing back all that's gone
Of rewinding the moments
I've moved on from
Of singing lyrics I've long forgotten
Is it just a soft passing breeze?

COBWEBS OF SILENCE

Yes, I'm stubborn
When it comes to melt
Easy ways to defend you
I've found each day and I've felt

Ruthless on paper sometimes
I'm not great at poetry
It's just God's grace to grant me
Confined space to be free

My pen shivers sometimes
Sometimes, my fingers do
Are they complex cobwebs of thoughts
Or silent ways to miss you?

THE BRIDGES

Distant, beautiful and strong
Those were the bridges I won
Brighter than the sunrays
Softer than the fog mist
They shone, somewhere out of the crowd
And there we sat hand on hand
That's where I remember we used to stand
Just like the bridges
Were the connections in us
Unbreakable trust, strangely woven
You and I were one strength
The bridge stands tall even now
But the connections have fallen apart
We grew to better, but not together
There's still some hope however
To see us stand connected
Tall over the bridge.

THE EPISTLE

A lot more than his expressions
Expressed his thoughts
A little deeper than the words
He formed in the empty clouds
Swung his beliefs in heights
A little shy he was
His hairs, constantly rattling
With the gone wind
A handful more did he think
Before he shared his things
The words of the epistle
Defined more than I should
Have known about him
I discovered a mountain in those words
Not a human soul in love.

RECALL

It's the middle of the night
Caffeine fills my soul so right
I can count on the streetlights
On the other side of
The blue window curtains
I can see the stars mounting
In the empty hollow sky
That resembles my existence
I can hear and overhear
The wolves in the woods
Far, far away
But I can't look out for you
Even after one thousand and one efforts
Ah! At least we share the same azure.

ANOTHER CUP

How about another cup
Of sugar and memories
That would add sweetness to centuries?
Of some bitterness and fight
And then soon erase all the plight?
Of some tiny glowing pearls
That circulates like my curls?
Of merry evenings with music
Meaningful verses and unknown rubric?
Of romantic moves around the fireplace
And bow down with pleasant grace?
Of the books with old perfumed pages
And bid a goodbye to all the dark ages?
Of blooming smiles that you reflect
Which is all that I'd endlessly recollect!

THERE WAS A GUY

There was a guy
And none knew him so well
People scared of his beard
Never understood his smile behind
He rose to heights with dedication
Seldom did he tire down like a setting sun
He beautified things that came his way
And grew wild for the achievements he craved
In a cacophony of wilderness
He always found a silent firewood
For his nature was of bubbling stream
And he could never stop running
Quivering ideas, his imagination ran wilder
That when he sat down on a rock
It portrayed afterlife
Transcending to various scenes
His torrents grew rapid
He wasn't afraid of hurricanes
The guy resembled luminous existence.

PRELUDES OF LOVE

Strolling through the forest
I hear dry leaves cracking under my feet
The glowing insects
Out of peace, they were out the street

Gradually the nature got me in its lap
On the path to tranquillity
All chirping followed by
The endless flow of a brook's fertility

Footsteps to finding peace
An owl kept staring at the nature's wonder
Seemed like the nature is looking for me
Clouds followed me and then the thunder

It was no unusual phenomenon
But an unusual feeling drove
The sky full of stars
Sing me preludes of love

It's another soul whom I know
Walking beside me like a lath
The sky guided us
Silently to our destined path.

Preludes of Love

Something sparkles at a distance
A firefly singing its freedom tale
Her eyes were glowing
Reflecting my dale.

The two clouds separate
Giving way to the moonlight
A pure joy in her eyes
Made my heart skip a beat

The firefly disappears
As the crescent made her black hair shine
And glowing glasses
Her footsteps in sync with mine.

I remove those glasses
To see the moon shine in her eyes
She smiles soft and gentle
As chilly winds and our faces form ties

The sound of the water in the brook
Made the existence clear
Of a thousand pebbles beneath
Feelings rush with a cheer

We get closer
My little finger touching hers
A new sense comes into being

Preludes of Love

And the rest blurs.

A whole new world
Unravels in front of me
The sound of the brook
Turns into a soft melody

A romantic tune paves a new way
Losing myself in a different beauty
I feel bright in the darkness
Right beside me, she was the key

It all flows endlessly
Just as the brook beside us
The brightness kept inculcating
Leaving behind all the pain we never chose

The cool breeze makes me closer
Holding hands, towards a new place of peace
We reach a peak where
Everything looked like a beautiful crease

Just as there is more of beauty
In the world of miseries
The gates to heaven itself
Is with the person beside me

Her hand is all the positivity
I ever needed to survive

Preludes of Love

Enough to cover up
All the negativity to thrive

Sitting down we watch the moon
Her head leaning on my shoulder
And she finds peace
She craved for since ages' border

With her presence
My night is a sunny dawn
Leaning towards her
My heart is then reborn

Spiritually surrounded we kiss
Her face in my hands
An everlasting influence followed
The brook's melody kept it alive in sands.

ETHEREAL

A hundred steps I pace
Lissom on your surface
Intertwining fingers and how they tilt
Storytelling palms, gracefully lilt
Toes together while we do the doffing
Like pretty ripples in the offing
Imbuing impressions of togetherness
Treading slow towards love and madness
Yet all is a plethora of past imperial
For it all ends being Ethereal.

UNHEARD EUPHONY

Unknown yet true
Is that voice inside you

Ages since that euphony stroke
Something deep inside me awoke

Blessed smile it was on hearing
Just as a dream gets its way clearing

Best part of you is that unknown beauty
Lucky is she, whose it's going to be the duty

That ringing laugh still covers my ear
Ages shall pass and boredom can't stop me hear

More than euphonium shines your euphony
Blessed as a soul, you're my destiny.

ARRIVAL OF THE DEPARTURE

Far that we were
Could only be that an imagination
Warmth of your arms
And pain of your tears in nation

The hug couldn't be everlasting
For intended it was to be the last
Owls awake and so were we
Tempest, moments running fast

To bid off forever
Enforced unwillingness to hear
Clouds unfolded secrets
At the beginning of the departure.

THE JOY FOREVER

Away from the hustling cities
You're a place to reach
A little flower to a giant tree
Your fragrance shores the sea beach

Descriptions fall apart
Coming back to you
Desirous connections my way
You're that soul so true

If a thing of beauty
Is a joy forever,
You're the beautiful gem
And the joy creator

Lines could never describe
A soul so humble and brave
Don't be sad, my older friend
I'll be accompanying you till your grave…

WALK A MILE IN MY SHOES

Walk a mile
In my shoes
See where they lead you
Hear whom they lead you
Verses in my ink
Dipped to linger
Empty-handed I shall vanish
All remains are the words for you
Tighten your toes
For they won't fit you
A little more do they pace up
When they find an empty mind
Don't be afraid
My destiny isn't too harsh
Roughly gets described with illness
But sometimes turns a star
Walk a mile
In my shoes…

THE ORCHID OF LOVE

The forest was dark
Damp trees and thorny bush
Flowers all dead
Forward I strived with a push

Looking for you, the orchid of love
Full of life, blooming alone
Far away where my footsteps followed
Red petals, unique you shone

Sun baked leaves cracked down,
there was no steam around
With withered lips I sang
The song of longing, soft and sound

The path was uneven
Pebbles shook me from within
Unquenched remained my thirst
Just like my love had been…

HALF PENNED VERSE

Half ink on the paper
Half blood in the heart
Just a little effort
That makes up a total me
Right from there, up the sky
The million stars appointed
To destine our meet
A sincere collision of hearts
Apart, far, far away
To reach what's beyond our reach
A little sacrifice
That makes up a total us
Right from there, down the ocean of depth
The hundred pearls beneath
That destine our togetherness
Far yet close
To hold what's invisible –
Half ink on the paper
Half blood in my heart...

PARALLEL UNIVERSE

There's a parallel universe,
I believe.
Where I love you
And you love me back
Where we have a connection
In our stars.

THE BOOK

Scented pages with yellow glimpses
My fingers occupied and pre-occupied
Turning them with the same enthusiasm
As yesterday and the day before
And the days earlier of hope
Silent smiles and silent tears
All being a natural part
Pages blooming and the pages nude
Pages burning and the pretty prelude
All of them reflecting the mankind
Eyes lost and consciousness regained
Mind's eye being fed the coffee seeds
A few hands empty and some with a mug
Feet covered with blankets and some on the rug
Curls making soft touches and lips oh lord!
All versions and colours of love bookmarked
When your memories this book unfolds!

NIGHT VISIONS

Fetching visions arrived me last night
Not mere hallucinations I pretend
But rather an escape into the reality
A hunch of the procrastinating end

He gifted me a wristwatch, arresting
And chattered quite impressive and subtle
As I showed my gratitude
His smiles behind the clouds were visible

Ours has been an inexpressible art
Unconsciously pounding in emptiness
Still and slow our roads parallel
And destiny helpless!

THE HEART IN TRANCE

Unclouded and irresponsibly bright
I wonder if I could make it alright

Poisonous swords flinching across my heart borders
Speak slow and safe, of the innocent murders

Traversing through the illusions and perplexities of life
A gentle disorder, on the artist's palette and baker's knife

I flip through the yellowed pages in the loft
And remark the bittersweet moments we had spent oft

Reminiscence engulfs me into heavenly pleasure
And tough it is to find out any more of leisure

Once, twice and all over again
I fall prey, a denial to sustain.

POTENTIAL MIST

Cause I wanna be your sunrise
The morning glow on your skin
Drifting to nowhere but around you
I'd stick to you through thick and thin

Your colourfu; body crucified evils
And the pure little soul blessed with innocence
Sins kept away and so did the sinners
Everyone fell for you, right at the fence

How that gusty wind quivered you, to dance
There were chords of my guitar string
Synchronizing your body and my souls
Tenacious, you beautified fresh every spring

Established on the grassy yard
Surrounded by your army – a dozen more
Little twigs and bigger shadows couldn't betray you
You smiled always – over sunshine or during downpour

I still remember the moon light mist
Gingerly landing on you
As I watched you slowly grow
With the drops of gentle dew.

Preludes of Love

Those curled yet proliferate petals
Were my source of joy
Out of home and back in,
They tied me up like Helen of Troy

Though there's more I'd get enticed to
It's all unexplainable what I really miss
In the wide world of terror and fear
Now that you've left me to the solitude bliss

No more magic stories do I weave
Guns and gore rampant all over the street
It's not just you who has dried and retired
But also, a part of me, my joy and discreet.

IN REMEMBRANCE

All these years
I've thrown out all my fears

Healing my scars quiet and pious
Without any sincere bias

Ever since you've entered into my life
I've grown into an independent strong rife

The millions of memories we've filled in jars
Shall shine brighter than all the stars

And no length of poetry would describe us the best
So let it be confined to us, an example for the rest!

www.ingramcontent.com/pod-product-compliance
Lightning Source LLC
LaVergne TN
LVHW050426160726
843469LV00041B/1248

* 9 7 8 9 3 5 4 3 8 3 0 1 4 *